Printed in the U.S.A.

ISBN 0-7172-8271-6

JIM HENSON'S MUPPETS
IN

Piggy for President

A Book About Friendship

By Ellen Weiss • Illustrated by Tom Brannon

GROLIER

The Extra-Cool After-School Club was hold-ing its very first elections. Everyone was ex-cited. Their new club was going to be so much fun!

"This meeting is called to order!" said Rowlf. Everyone stopped talking and looked at him.

"What we have to do first," he went on, "is decide who's running for office. Who wants to be treasurer?"

"I do!" said Janice. "I'm good with money."

"Does anyone else want to be treasurer?" Rowlf asked. No one did, so Janice was elected.

Rowlf volunteered to be secretary, and everyone happily agreed that he would be great for the job.

"Now," said Rowlf, "who should be president?"
"Kermit!" Fozzie sang out.
"Piggy!" Skeeter said at the same time.

Rowlf nodded. "Okay," he said. "That means we'll have to vote. Whoever gets the most votes will become our new president."

The club members decided that the election would be held in a week, on the next Tuesday.

After the meeting, Kermit and Piggy walked home together.

"It's going to be strange running for president against my best friend," said Piggy.

"I know," said Kermit. "It's strange for me, too. But it's okay. I won't mind if you win. You'll make a good president."

"I feel the same way," said Piggy. "I won't mind if you win. But"—she paused for a moment—"I do really want to be president."

"So do I," admitted Kermit.

"Well, may the best person win," said Piggy. And they shook hands.

All that week, Piggy and Kermit cam-
paigned.

On Wednesday, Gonzo, Skeeter, and Janice
came over to Piggy's house and helped her
make posters.

That afternoon, Piggy went over to the clubhouse to hang up the posters. Kermit and Fozzie were already there.

"Kermit and I made these posters this morning," said Fozzie.

"I like them," said Piggy. "Especially the green one."

On Thursday, Piggy went to the library. "Do you have any books about campaign speeches?" she whispered to the librarian. "You know, speeches you give when you run for president."

"Third aisle on the left," whispered the librarian.

There, sitting on the floor in the third aisle, was Kermit. When he looked up and saw Piggy, they both burst out laughing.

"Sssssh!" scolded the librarian.

On Monday, the day before the election, the candidates gave speeches at a special club meeting. "If I am elected," declared Piggy, "we will put on a show. With music. And we'll hold a great big party in the school gym. And we'll paint the clubhouse wonderful colors."

"Great ideas," said everybody.

Then Kermit gave his speech. "If I'm elected president," said Kermit, "we'll clean up the litter in the park. And we'll have bike races. And we'll also have a bake sale to raise money to buy books for kids in the hospital."

"Also great ideas," said everybody.

On Tuesday morning, Piggy woke up feeling excited. *I wonder who'll be the winner?* she thought. She started counting on her fingers. *Probably Gonzo and Skeeter and Janice will vote for me. And I'll vote for myself. That's four.*

Then she thought about Kermit's votes. *Fozzie for sure,* she mused. *And Rowlf and Scooter, I'll bet. And of course, Kermit will vote for himself. Hmmm, that's four, too. Maybe we'll have a tie.*

All day long, Piggy was surprised to find herself thinking about Kermit. *Kermit wants to be president so much*, she thought. *And he'd be a good president. A bake sale and bike races and cleaning up the park are wonderful ideas.*

And Kermit is such a good friend to me, she thought. *He's always there when I need him. He always forgives me if I hurt his feelings. Sometimes he even gives up things for me, like the day I had the chicken pox and he missed a class trip to keep me company.*

The more Piggy thought about it, the more she realized what a special friend Kermit was.

As voting time grew near, Piggy made a decision. She would vote for Kermit. The tie would be broken, and Kermit would win.

Piggy was smiling as she put her ballot into the box.

That night, Rowlf, as club secretary, counted the votes. "One for Piggy," he said. "One for Kermit. Two more for Piggy. One for Kermit. One for Piggy. Two for Kermit. That's four votes each," he finally proclaimed. "It's a tie!"

Piggy was very surprised. Kermit should have won! Had she counted wrong?

She looked over at him. He was standing there, looking just as surprised.

"What do we do now?" Skeeter asked.

"Maybe we should have another election," Fozzie suggested.

"But it will just come out the same," Scooter said, and everyone had to agree.

"Well," Rowlf said slowly. "Kermit and Piggy both have good ideas. Why can't they share the job?"

"Great idea!" everyone agreed.

The next day, Piggy was on line in the school lunchroom. Kermit and Rowlf were a little bit ahead of her, so they didn't see her. She couldn't help overhearing what they were talking about.

"...that was amazing," Rowlf was saying. "I thought you would win for sure."

"I'll tell you a secret," Kermit said. "I thought Piggy would win. You see, I voted for her."

"You did?" Rowlf asked. "How come?"

"Well, I thought about what a good friend Piggy is to me," said Kermit, "and about how she always cheers me up. And I thought about how much she wanted to be president. Plus, I liked her ideas. So I decided to vote for her."

Piggy went flying over to Kermit and gave him a big hug. "You voted for me?" she said. "I voted for you!"

"You did?" A big smile came over Kermit's face. "No wonder there was a tie!"

"So," Piggy said, "what should we do first?"

"We'll put on a show—" Kermit began.

"—to raise money to buy books for kids in the hospital!" finished Piggy.

"Great!" Rowlf chimed in. "Let's get started!"

Let's Talk About Friendship

Piggy and Kermit both did something very special when they voted for each other for club president. And it made them feel great, because it let them know how much they care about one another.

Here are some questions about friendship for you to think about:

Who are your friends?

What are some of the things you like about them?

Have you ever done something special for a friend? What was it? How did it make you feel?